THE FORCE AWAKENS: VOLUME 3

Luke Skywalker has vanished. In his absence, the sinister First Order has risen from the ashes of the Empire and will not rest until the last Jedi has been destroyed. The First Order and the Resistance are in desperate search for a map leading directly to Skywalker that is hidden inside the Resistance droid BB-8.

After Finn, a former stormtrooper, escapes the First Order, he crash-lands on Jakku where Rey, a young scavenger, has found BB-8. Rey, Finn, and BB-8 become allies and hijack the Millennium Falcon *to escape Jakku and the pursuing First Order.*

Once in space, however, the three find themselves caught by none other than smugglers Han Solo and Chewbacca, who in turn are being pursued by the Guavian Death Gang for a deal gone wrong. That is, until Han's cargo escapes....

CHUCK WENDIG
Writer

MARC LAMING
Artist

FRANK MARTIN
Colorist

VC's CLAYTON COWLES
Letterer

MIKE DEODATO & FRANK MARTIN
Cover Artists

HEATHER ANTOS
Editor

JORDAN D. WHITE
Supervising Editor

C.B. CEBULSKI
Executive Editor

AXEL ALONSO
Editor In Chief

JOE QUESADA
Chief Creative Officer

DAN BUCKLEY
Publisher

Based on the screenplay by
LAWRENCE KASDAN & J.J. ABRAMS
and
MICHAEL ARNDT

For Lucasfilm:
Creative Director MICHAEL SIGLAIN
Senior Editor FRANK PARISI
Lucasfilm Story Group RAYNE ROBERTS, PABLO HIDALGO, LELAND CHEE, MATT MARTIN

ABDO Spotlight

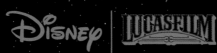

ABDOPUBLISHING.COM

Reinforced library bound edition published in 2018 by Spotlight,
a division of ABDO, PO Box 398166, Minneapolis, Minnesota 55439.
Spotlight produces high-quality reinforced library bound editions for
schools and libraries. Published by agreement with Marvel Characters, Inc.

Printed in the United States of America, North Mankato, Minnesota.
042017
092017

 THIS BOOK CONTAINS
RECYCLED MATERIALS

marvelkids.com

PUBLISHER'S CATALOGING IN PUBLICATION DATA

Names: Wendig, Chuck, author. | Ross, Luke ; Martin, Frank ; Laming, Marc,
   illustrators.
Title: The force awakens / writer: Chuck Wendig ; art: Luke Ross ; Frank Martin ;
   Marc Laming.
Description: Reinforced library bound edition. | Minneapolis, Minnesota : Spotlight,
   2018. | Series: Star wars : the force awakens | Volumes 1, 2, 4, 5, and 6 written
   by Chuck Wendig ; illustrated by Luke Ross & Frank Martin. | Volume 3 written
   by Chuck Wendig ; illustrated by Marc Laming & Frank Martin.
Summary: Three decades after the Rebel Alliance destroyed the Galactic Empire, a
   stirring in the Force brings young scavenger Rey, deserting Stormtrooper Finn,
   ace pilot Poe, and dark apprentice Kylo Ren's lives crashing together as the
   awakening begins.
Identifiers: LCCN 2016961930 | ISBN 9781532140228 (volume 1) | ISBN
   9781532140235 (volume 2) | ISBN 9781532140242 (volume 3) | ISBN
   9781532140259 (volume 4) | ISBN 9781532140266 (volume 5) | ISBN
   9781532140273 (volume 6)
Subjects: LCSH: Star Wars fiction--Comic book, strips, etc.--Juvenile fiction. |
   Space warfare--Juvenile fiction. | Adventure and adventurers--Juvenile fiction. |
   Graphic novels--Juvenile fiction.
Classification: DDC 741.5--dc23
LC record available at https://lccn.loc.gov/2016961930

Spotlight

A Division of ABDO
abdopublishing.com

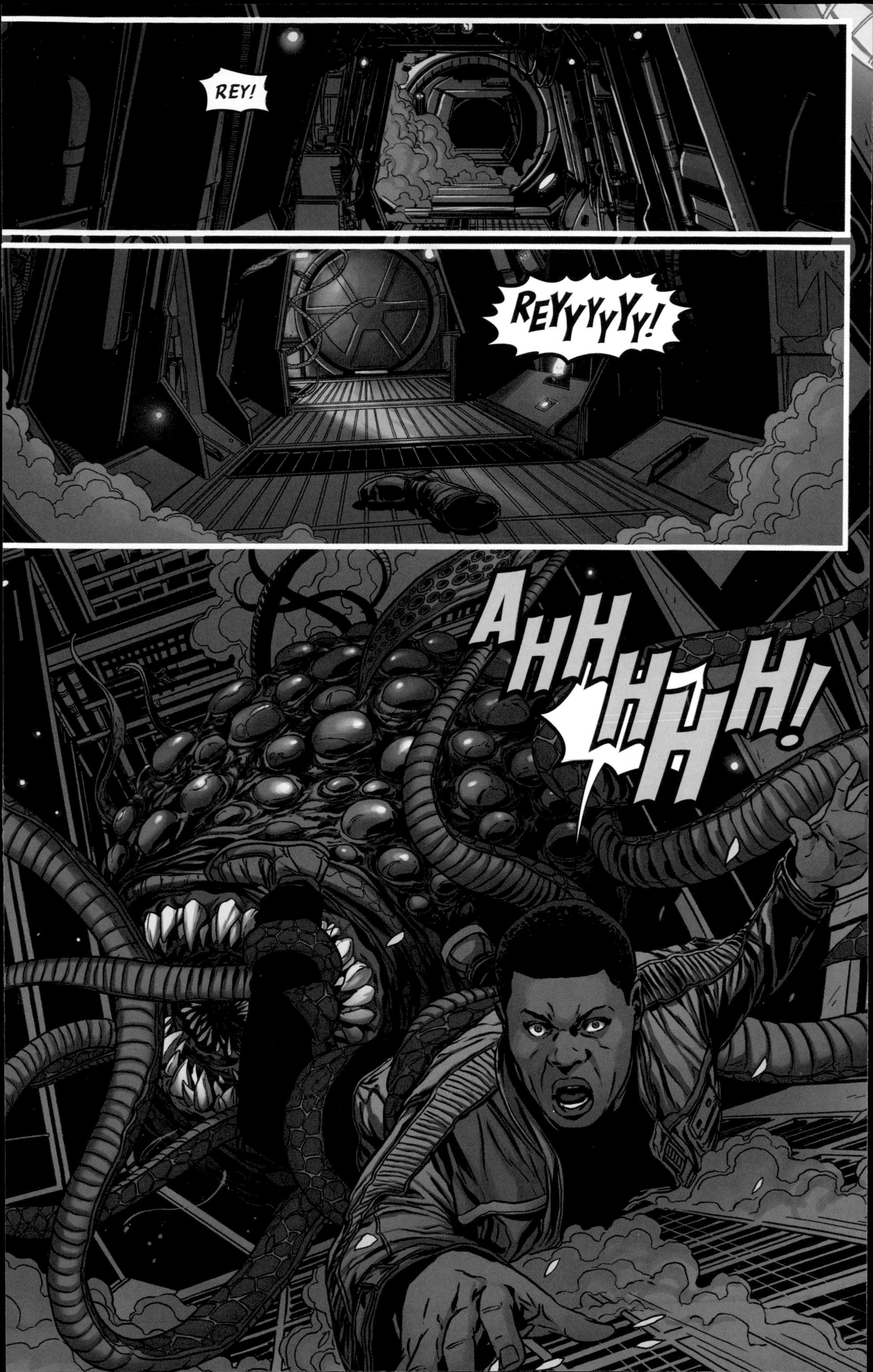
REY!
REYYYYYY!
AHHHHHH!

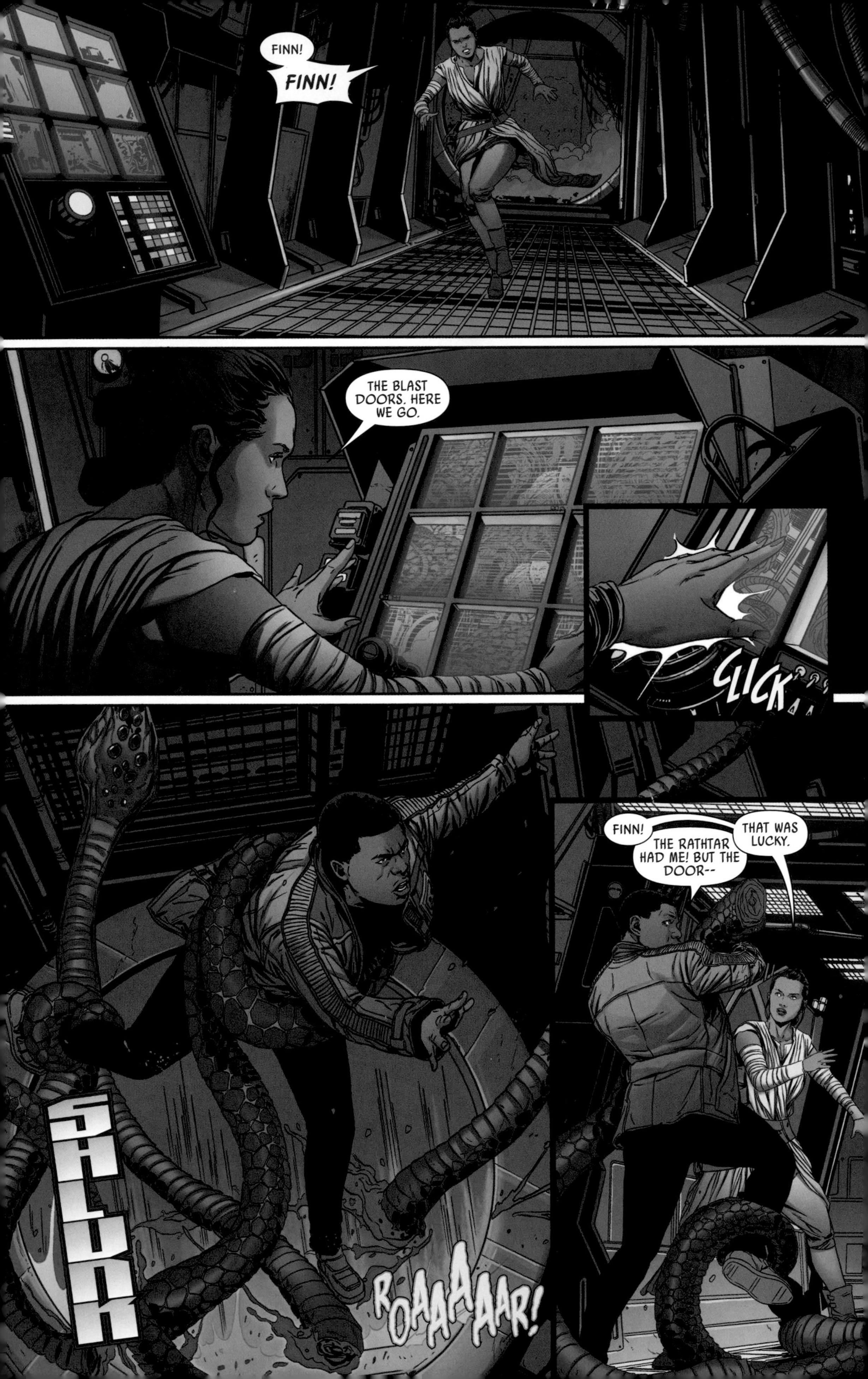
FINN!
FINN!
THE BLAST DOORS. HERE WE GO.
CLICK
SHLUNK
ROAAAAAR!
FINN!
THE RATHTAR HAD ME! BUT THE DOOR--
THAT WAS LUCKY.

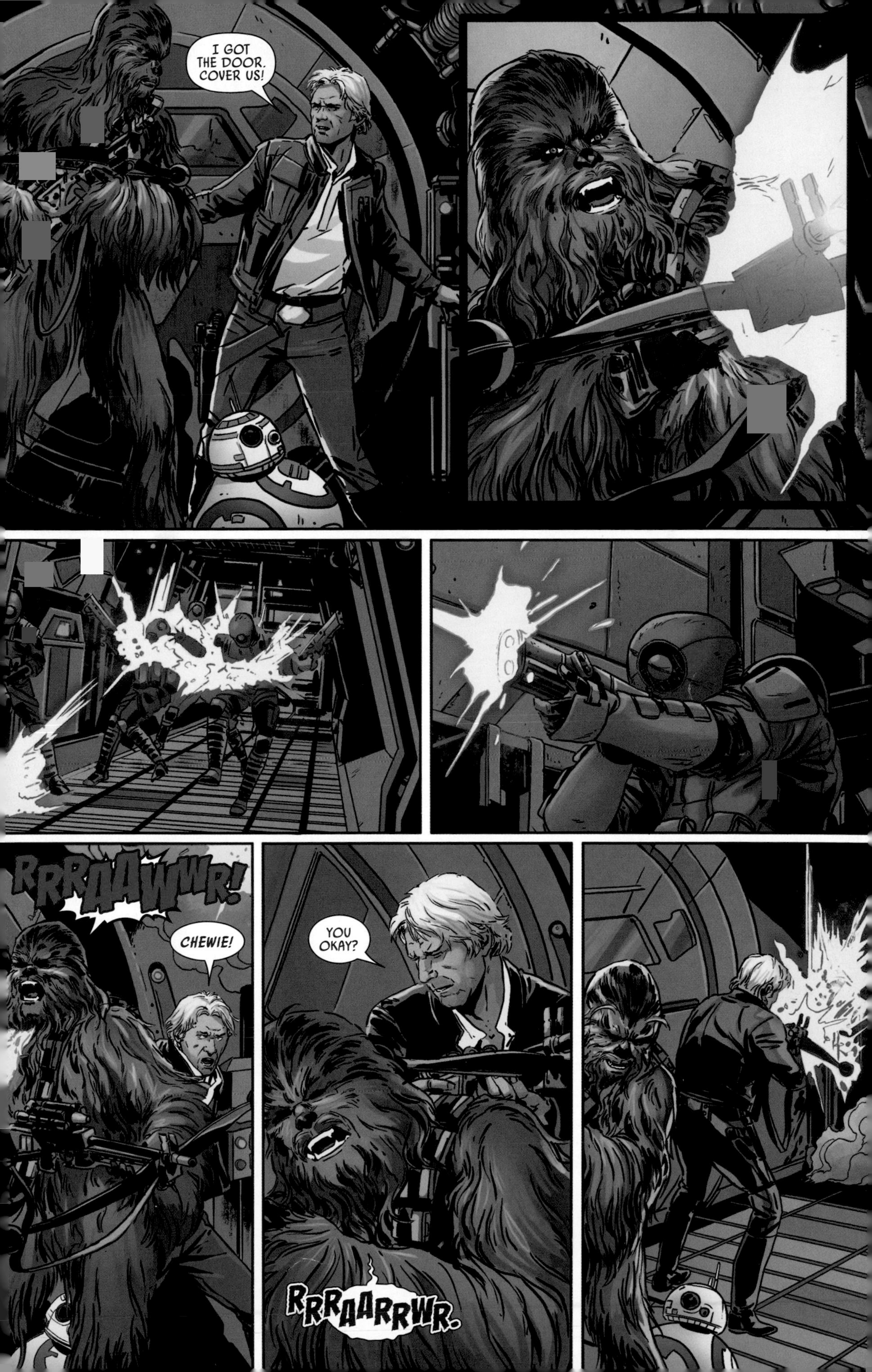
I GOT THE DOOR. COVER US!
RRRAAWWR!
CHEWIE!
YOU OKAY?
RRRAARRWR.

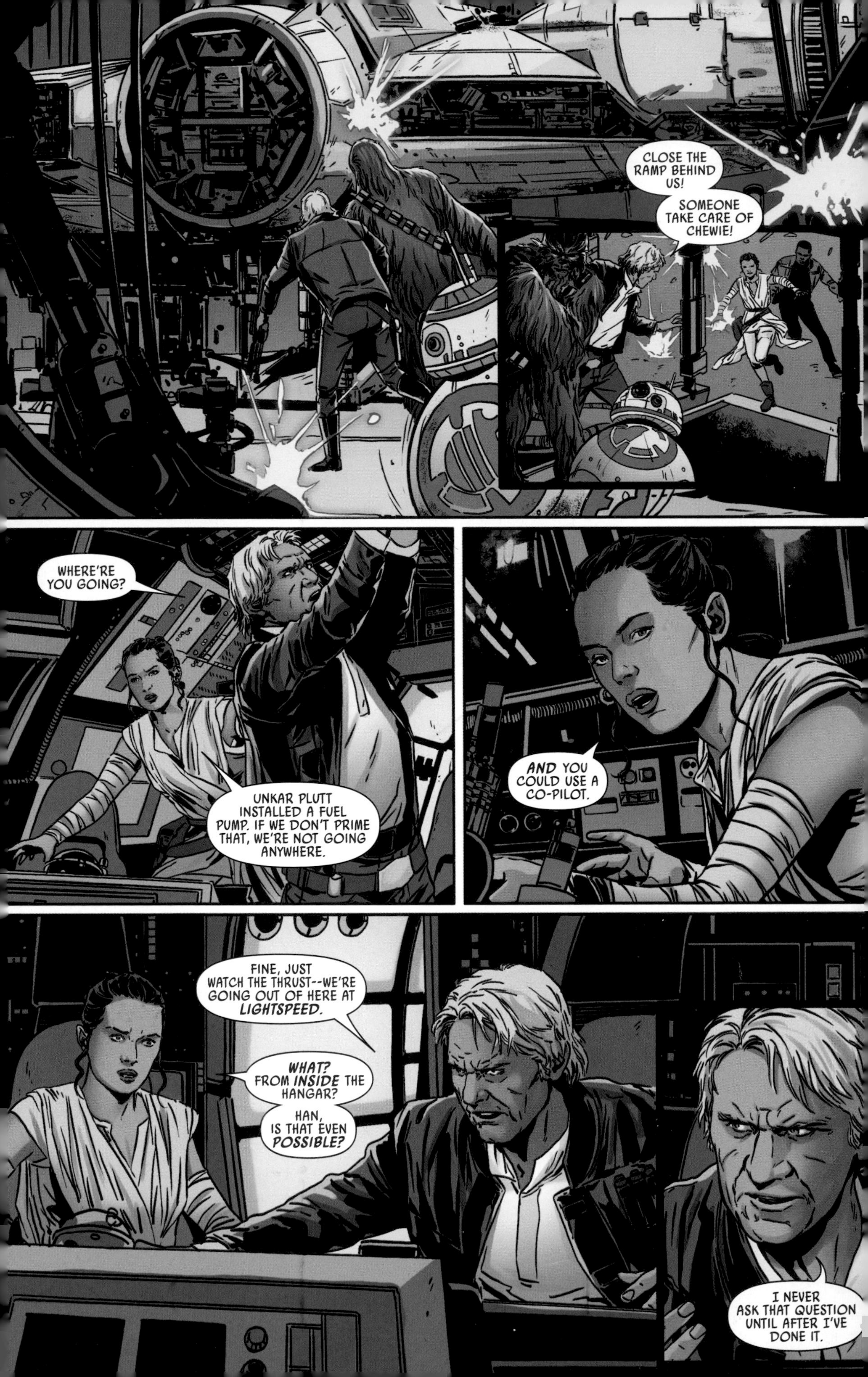
CLOSE THE RAMP BEHIND US!
SOMEONE TAKE CARE OF CHEWIE!
WHERE'RE YOU GOING?
UNKAR PLUTT INSTALLED A FUEL PUMP. IF WE DON'T PRIME THAT, WE'RE NOT GOING ANYWHERE.
AND YOU COULD USE A CO-PILOT.
FINE, JUST WATCH THE THRUST--WE'RE GOING OUT OF HERE AT LIGHTSPEED.
WHAT? FROM INSIDE THE HANGAR?
HAN, IS THAT EVEN POSSIBLE?
I NEVER ASK THAT QUESTION UNTIL AFTER I'VE DONE IT.

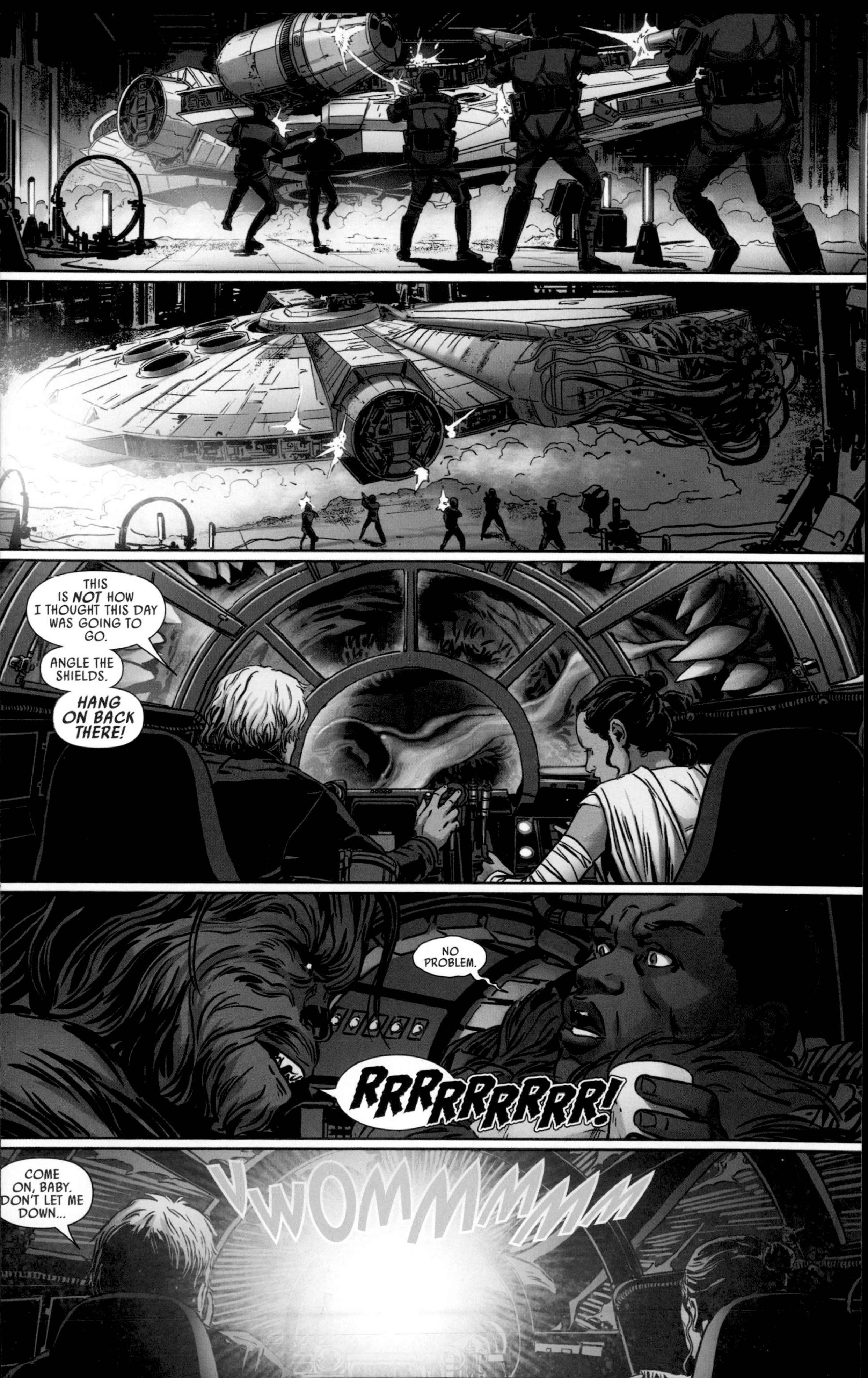

THIS IS NOT HOW I THOUGHT THIS DAY WAS GOING TO GO.
ANGLE THE SHIELDS.
HANG ON BACK THERE!
NO PROBLEM.
RRRRRRRRR!
COME ON, BABY. DON'T LET ME DOWN...
VWOMMMMM

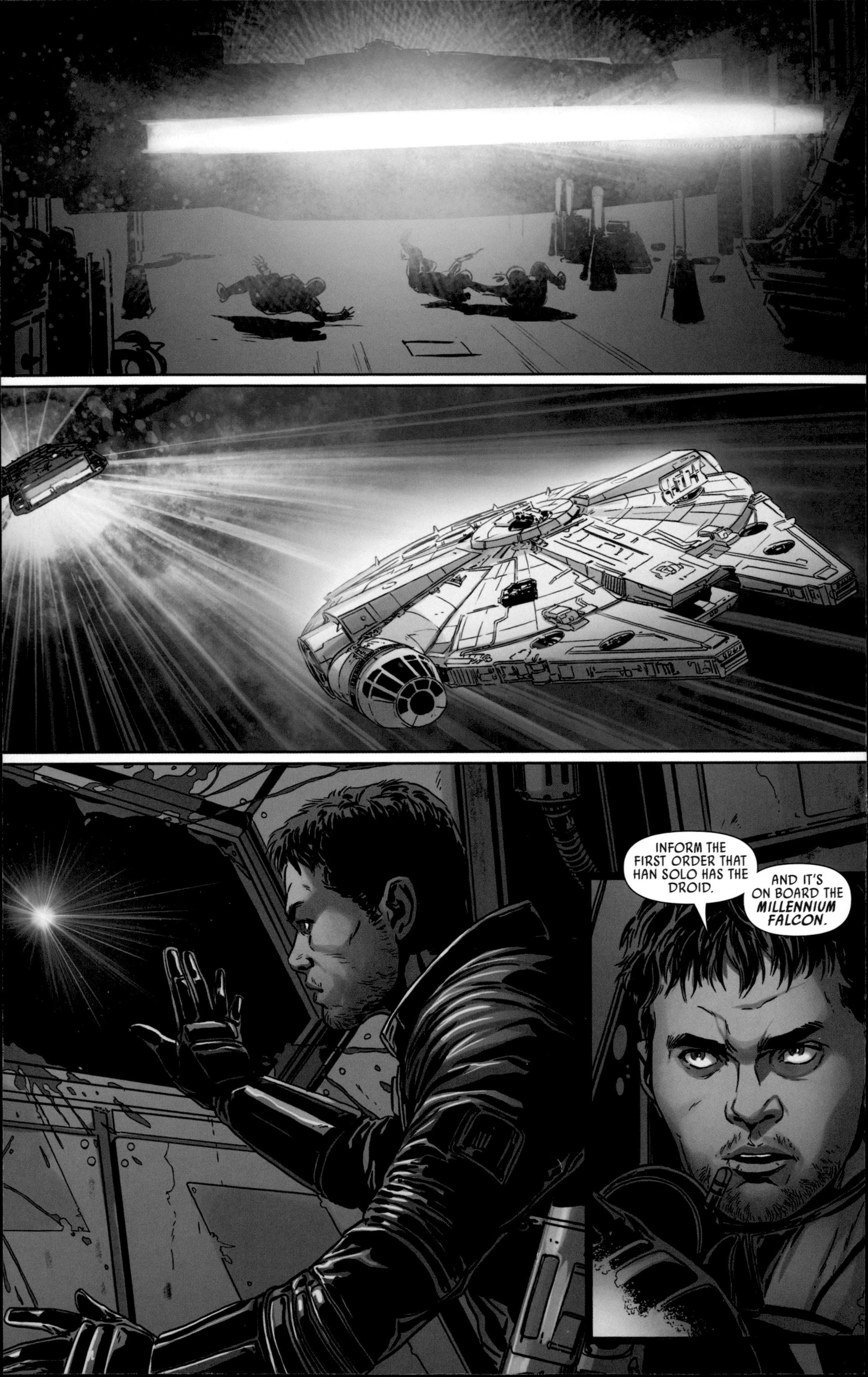
INFORM THE FIRST ORDER THAT HAN SOLO HAS THE DROID.
AND IT'S ON BOARD THE *MILLENNIUM FALCON*.

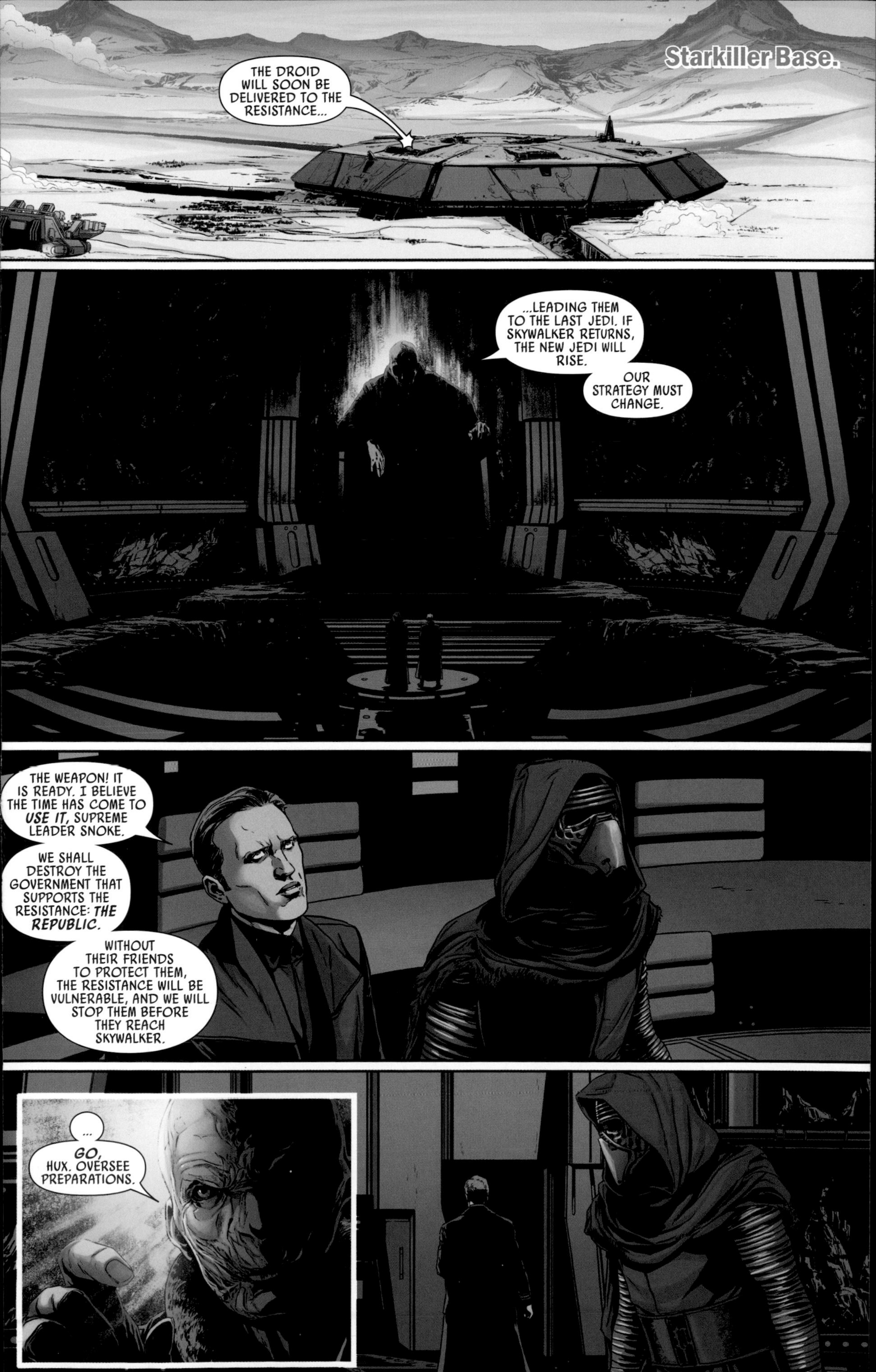
Starkiller Base.
THE DROID WILL SOON BE DELIVERED TO THE RESISTANCE...
...LEADING THEM TO THE LAST JEDI. IF SKYWALKER RETURNS, THE NEW JEDI WILL RISE.
OUR STRATEGY MUST CHANGE.
THE WEAPON! IT IS READY. I BELIEVE THE TIME HAS COME TO *USE IT*, SUPREME LEADER SNOKE.
WE SHALL DESTROY THE GOVERNMENT THAT SUPPORTS THE RESISTANCE: ***THE REPUBLIC.***
WITHOUT THEIR FRIENDS TO PROTECT THEM, THE RESISTANCE WILL BE VULNERABLE, AND WE WILL STOP THEM BEFORE THEY REACH SKYWALKER.
...
GO, HUX. OVERSEE PREPARATIONS.

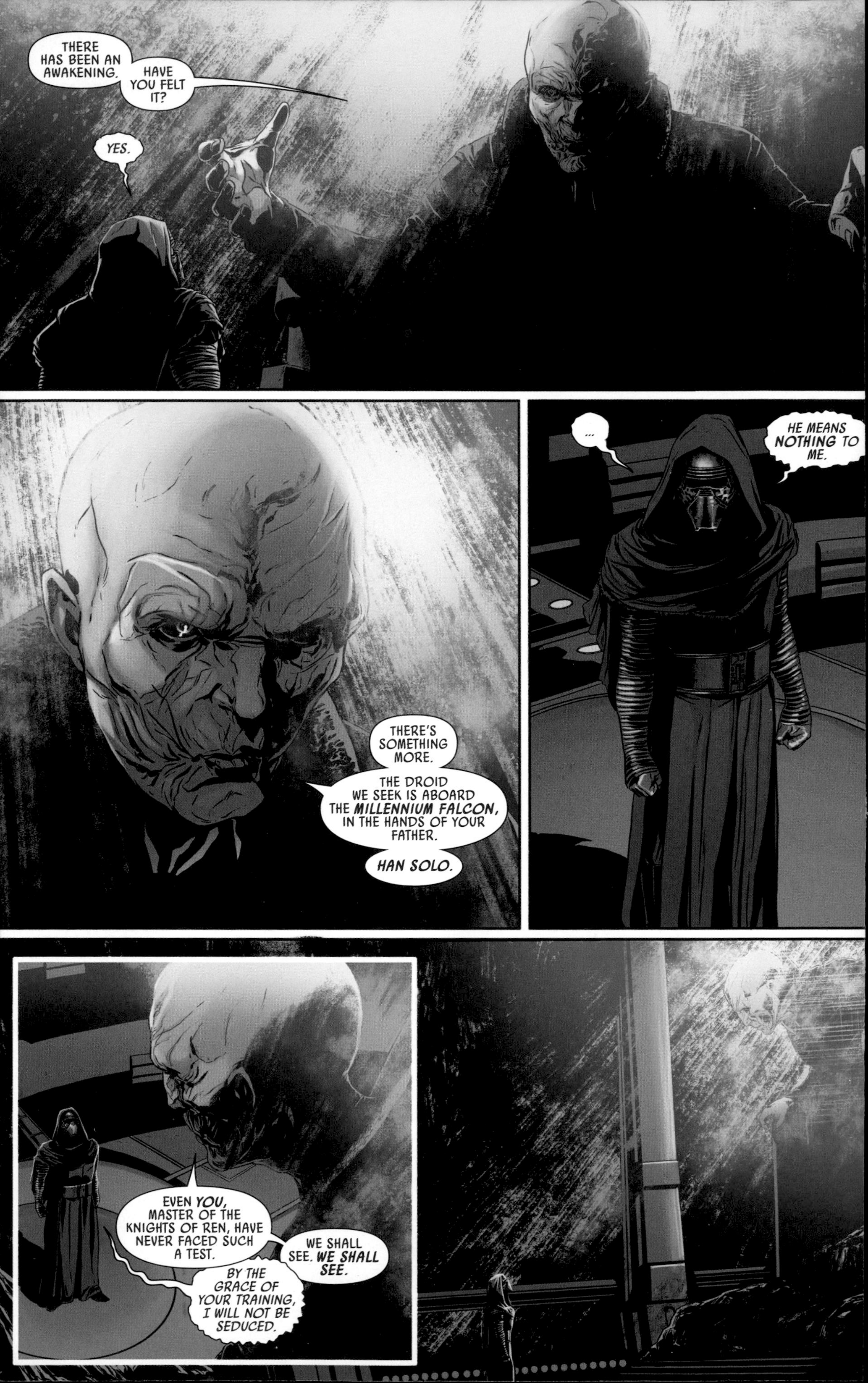

THERE HAS BEEN AN AWAKENING.
HAVE YOU FELT IT?
YES.
THERE'S SOMETHING MORE.
THE DROID WE SEEK IS ABOARD THE MILLENNIUM FALCON, IN THE HANDS OF YOUR FATHER.
HAN SOLO.
...
HE MEANS NOTHING TO ME.
EVEN YOU, MASTER OF THE KNIGHTS OF REN, HAVE NEVER FACED SUCH A TEST.
BY THE GRACE OF YOUR TRAINING, I WILL NOT BE SEDUCED.
WE SHALL SEE. WE SHALL SEE.

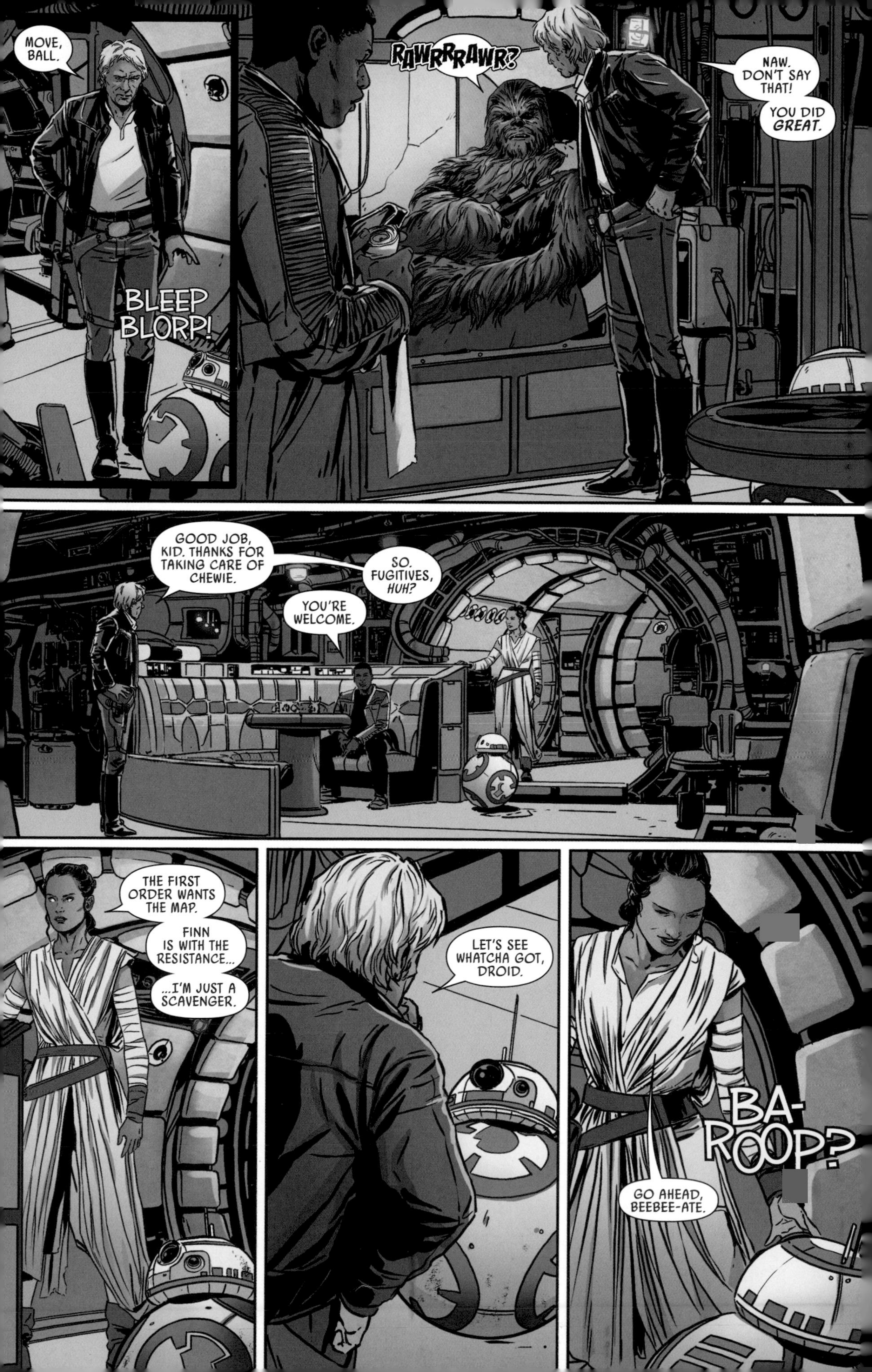
MOVE, BALL.
BLEEP BLORP!
RAWRRRAWR?
NAW. DON'T SAY THAT!
YOU DID GREAT.
GOOD JOB, KID. THANKS FOR TAKING CARE OF CHEWIE.
YOU'RE WELCOME.
SO. FUGITIVES, HUH?
THE FIRST ORDER WANTS THE MAP.
FINN IS WITH THE RESISTANCE...
...I'M JUST A SCAVENGER.
LET'S SEE WHATCHA GOT, DROID.
BA-ROOP?
GO AHEAD, BEEBEE-ATE.

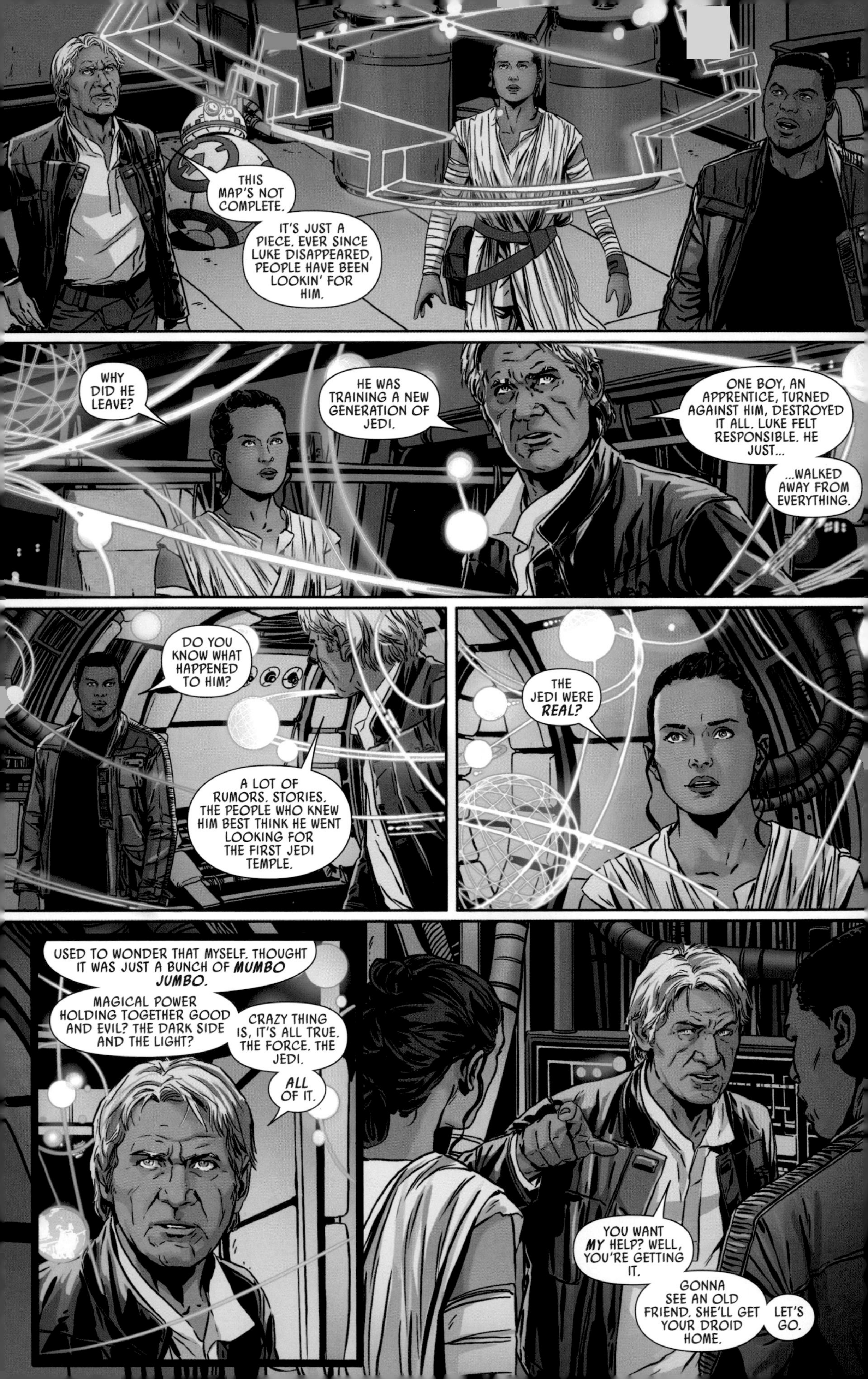
THIS MAP'S NOT COMPLETE.
IT'S JUST A PIECE. EVER SINCE LUKE DISAPPEARED, PEOPLE HAVE BEEN LOOKIN' FOR HIM.
WHY DID HE LEAVE?
HE WAS TRAINING A NEW GENERATION OF JEDI.
ONE BOY, AN APPRENTICE, TURNED AGAINST HIM, DESTROYED IT ALL. LUKE FELT RESPONSIBLE. HE JUST...
...WALKED AWAY FROM EVERYTHING.
DO YOU KNOW WHAT HAPPENED TO HIM?
A LOT OF RUMORS. STORIES. THE PEOPLE WHO KNEW HIM BEST THINK HE WENT LOOKING FOR THE FIRST JEDI TEMPLE.
THE JEDI WERE *REAL?*
USED TO WONDER THAT MYSELF. THOUGHT IT WAS JUST A BUNCH OF *MUMBO JUMBO*.
MAGICAL POWER HOLDING TOGETHER GOOD AND EVIL? THE DARK SIDE AND THE LIGHT?
CRAZY THING IS, IT'S ALL TRUE. THE FORCE. THE JEDI.
ALL OF IT.
YOU WANT *MY* HELP? WELL, YOU'RE GETTING IT.
GONNA SEE AN OLD FRIEND. SHE'LL GET YOUR DROID HOME.
LET'S GO.

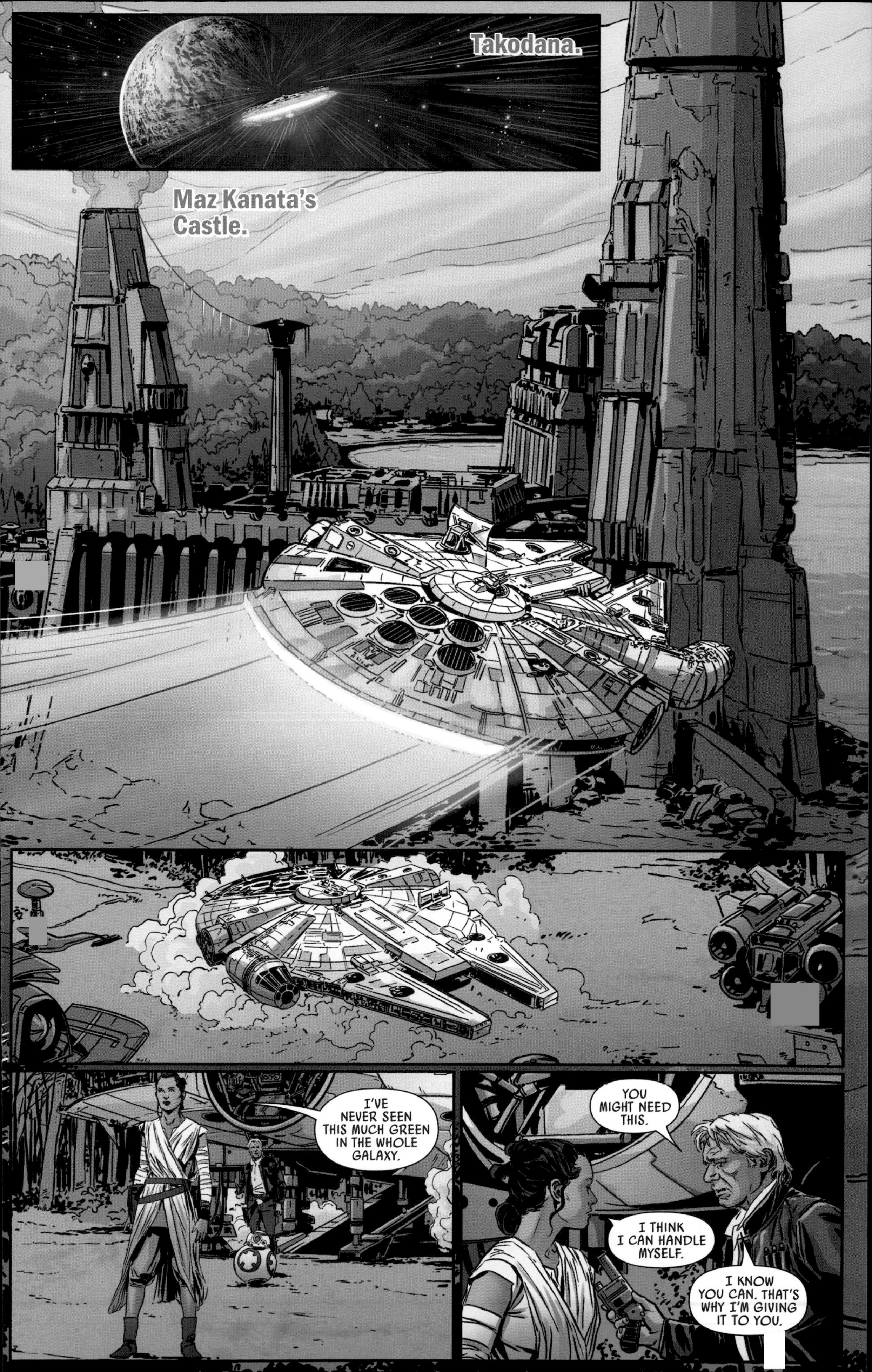
Takodana.
Maz Kanata's Castle.
I'VE NEVER SEEN THIS MUCH GREEN IN THE WHOLE GALAXY.
YOU MIGHT NEED THIS.
I THINK I CAN HANDLE MYSELF.
I KNOW YOU CAN. THAT'S WHY I'M GIVING IT TO YOU.

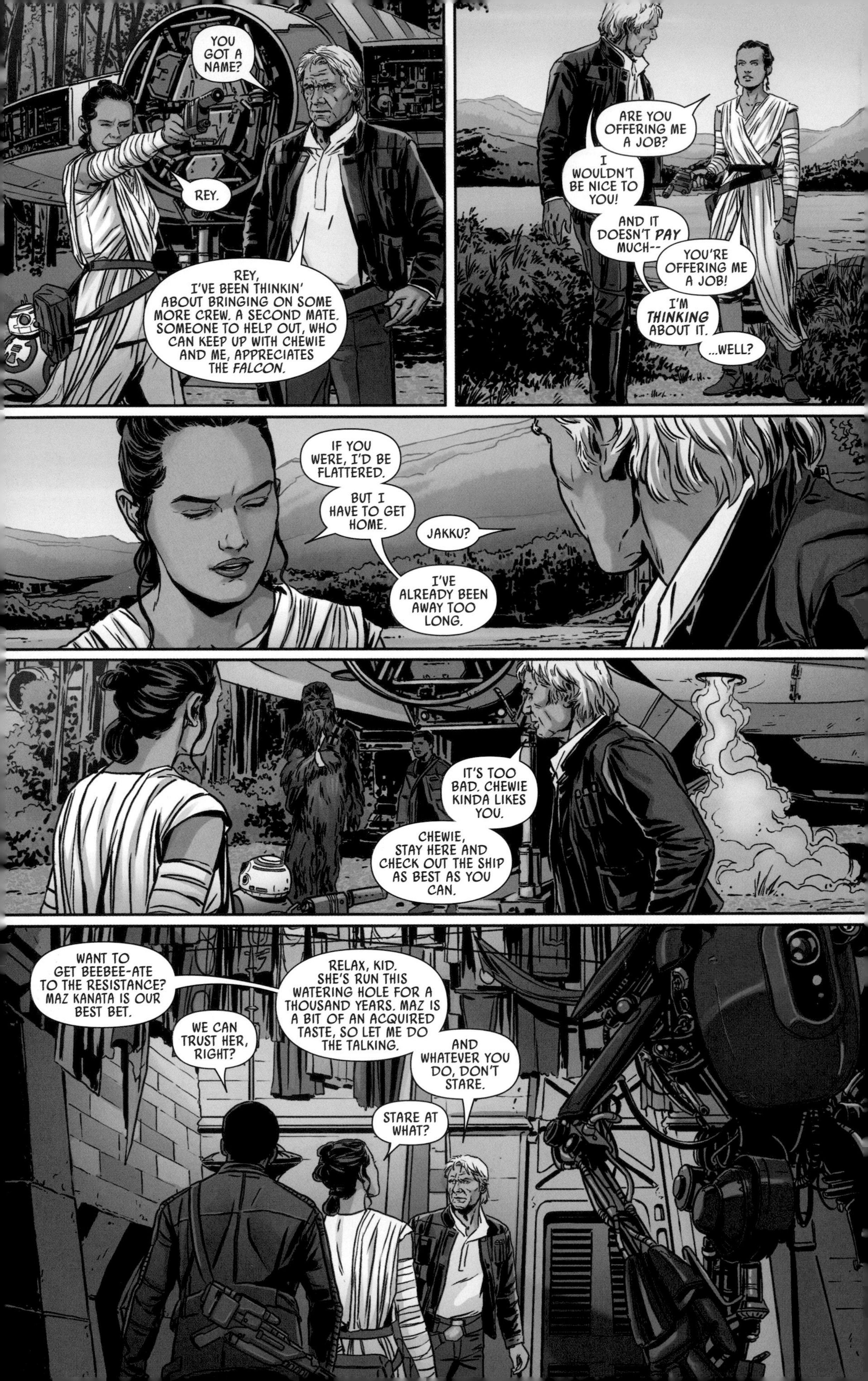
YOU GOT A NAME?
REY.
REY, I'VE BEEN THINKIN' ABOUT BRINGING ON SOME MORE CREW. A SECOND MATE. SOMEONE TO HELP OUT, WHO CAN KEEP UP WITH CHEWIE AND ME, APPRECIATES THE *FALCON*.
ARE YOU OFFERING ME A JOB?
I WOULDN'T BE NICE TO YOU!
AND IT DOESN'T *PAY* MUCH--
YOU'RE OFFERING ME A JOB!
I'M *THINKING* ABOUT IT.
...WELL?
IF YOU WERE, I'D BE FLATTERED.
BUT I HAVE TO GET HOME.
JAKKU?
I'VE ALREADY BEEN AWAY TOO LONG.
IT'S TOO BAD. CHEWIE KINDA LIKES YOU.
CHEWIE, STAY HERE AND CHECK OUT THE SHIP AS BEST AS YOU CAN.
WANT TO GET BEEBEE-ATE TO THE RESISTANCE? MAZ KANATA IS OUR BEST BET.
WE CAN TRUST HER, RIGHT?
RELAX, KID. SHE'S RUN THIS WATERING HOLE FOR A THOUSAND YEARS. MAZ IS A BIT OF AN ACQUIRED TASTE, SO LET ME DO THE TALKING.
AND WHATEVER YOU DO, DON'T STARE.
STARE AT WHAT?

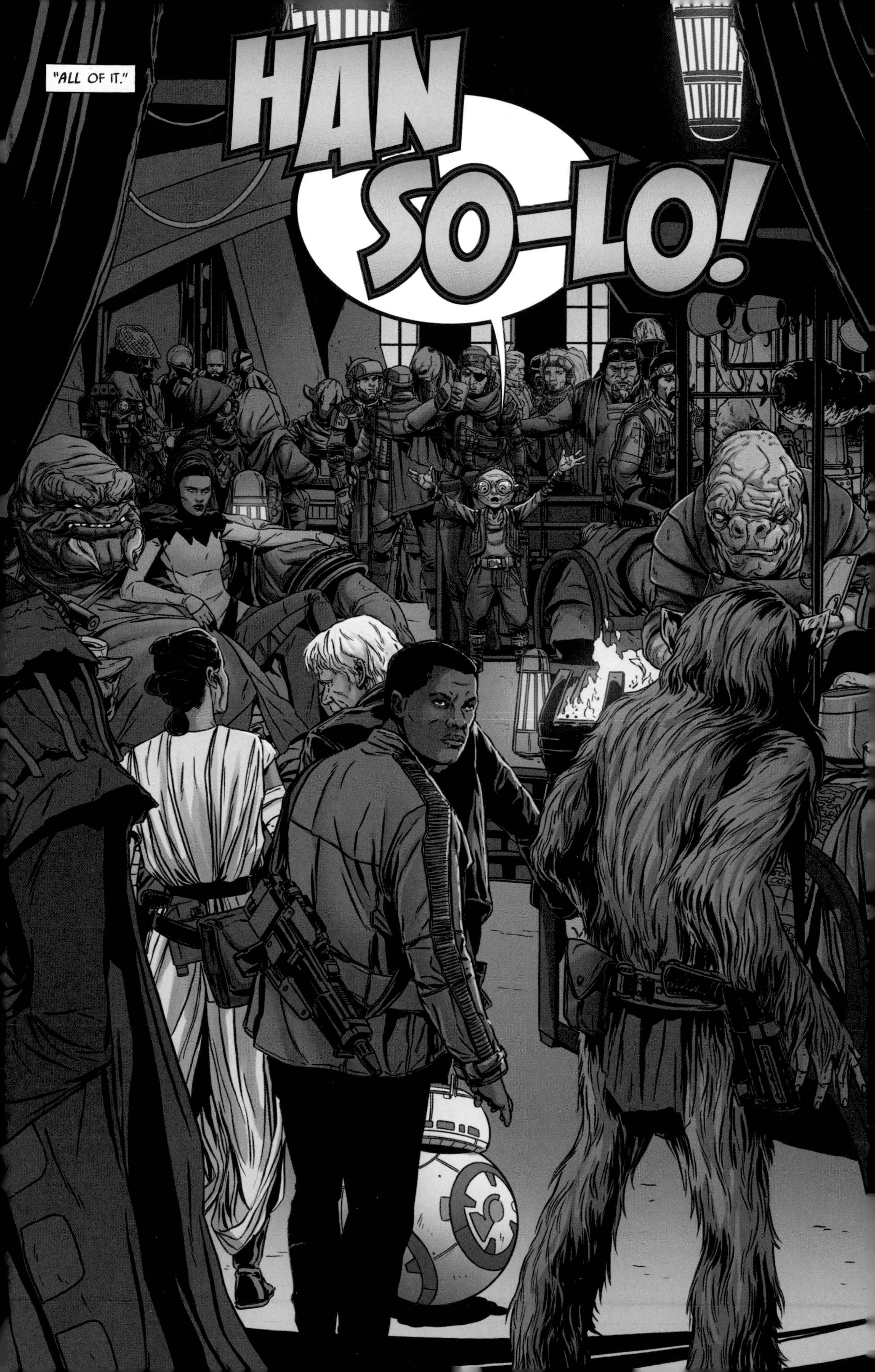
"ALL OF IT."
HAN SO-LO!

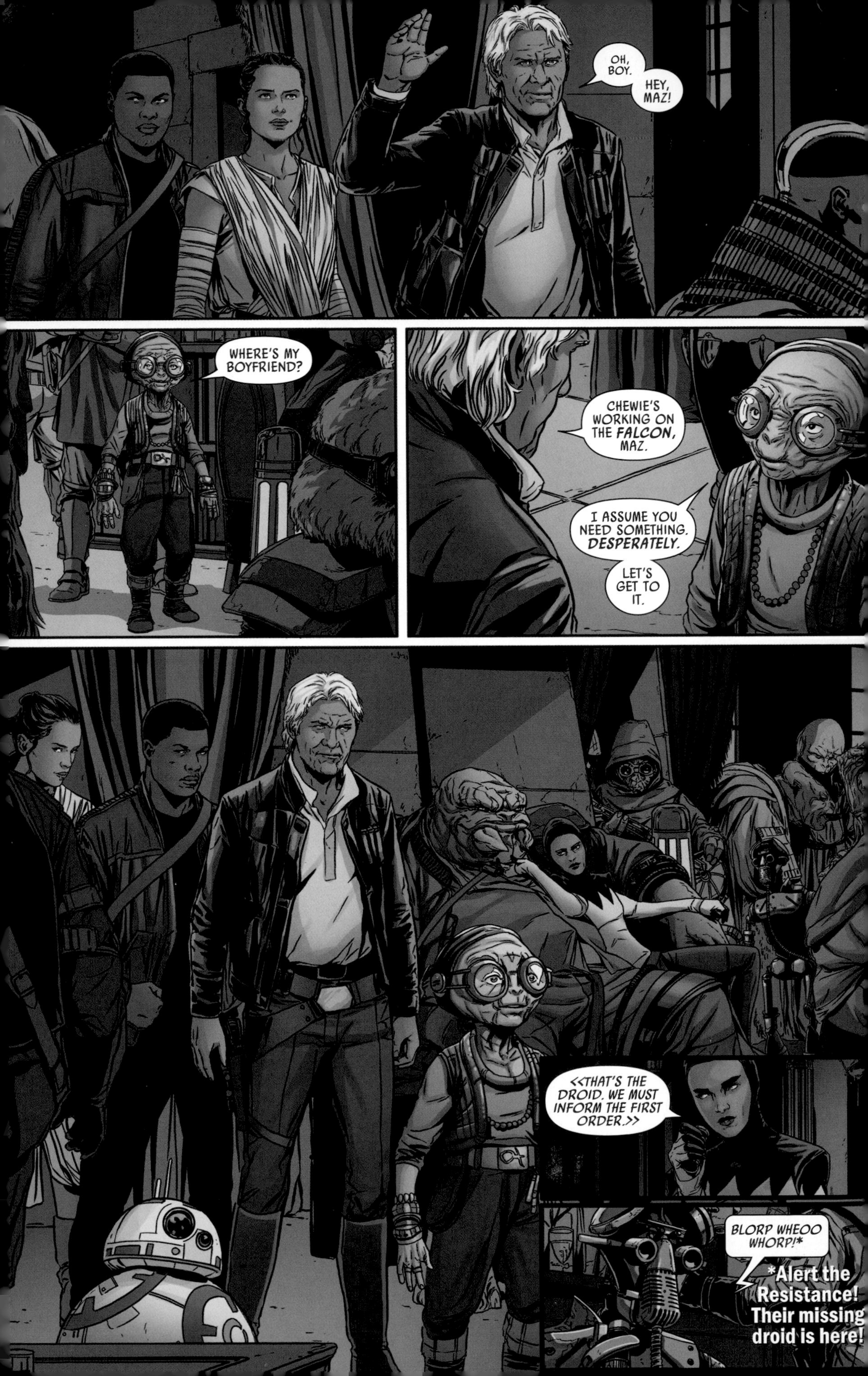
OH, BOY.
HEY, MAZ!
WHERE'S MY BOYFRIEND?
CHEWIE'S WORKING ON THE FALCON, MAZ.
I ASSUME YOU NEED SOMETHING. DESPERATELY.
LET'S GET TO IT.
<<THAT'S THE DROID. WE MUST INFORM THE FIRST ORDER.>>
BLORP WHEOO WHORP!*
*Alert the Resistance! Their missing droid is here!

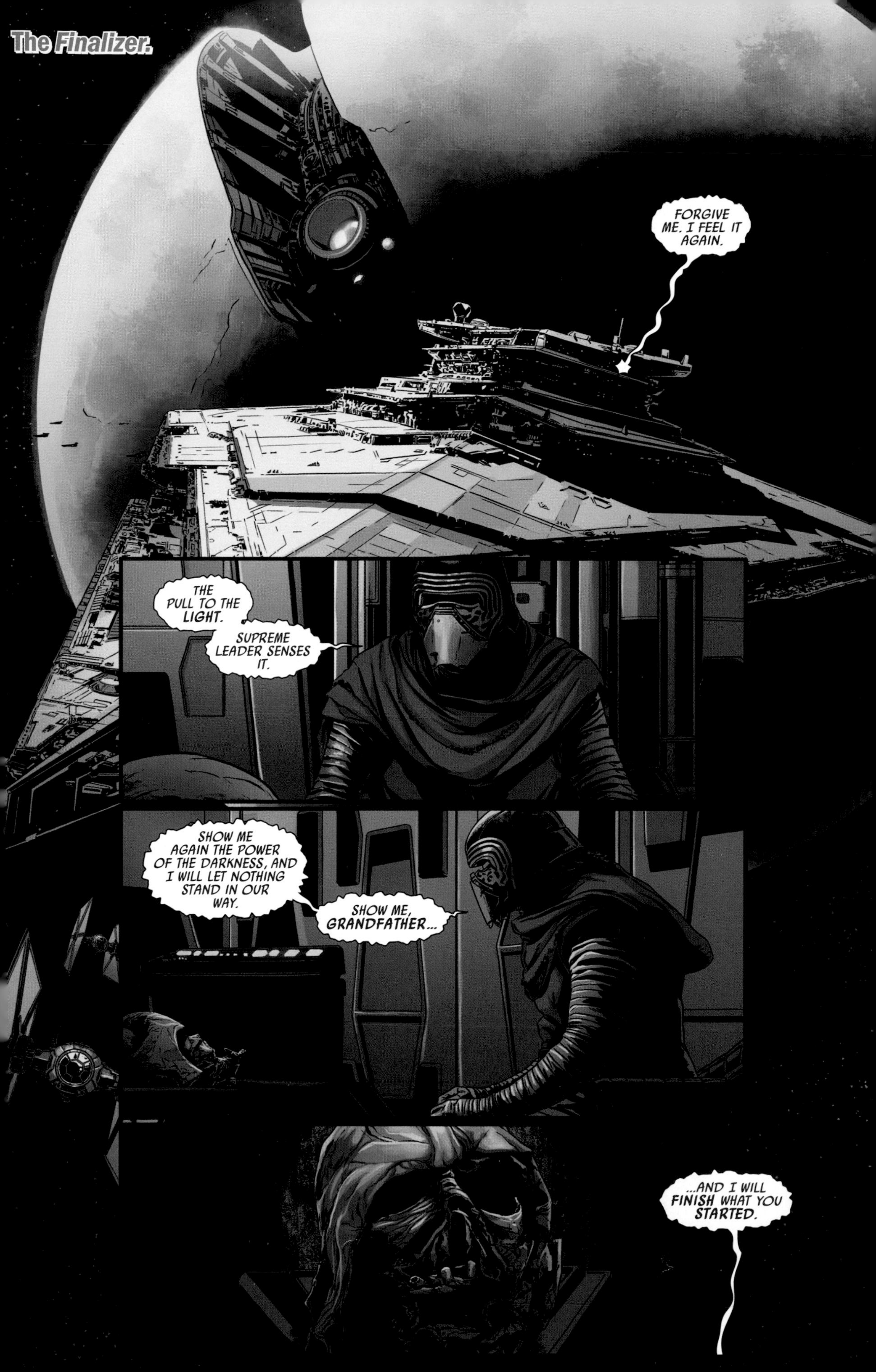

The Finalizer.
FORGIVE ME. I FEEL IT AGAIN.
THE PULL TO THE LIGHT.
SUPREME LEADER SENSES IT.
SHOW ME AGAIN THE POWER OF THE DARKNESS, AND I WILL LET NOTHING STAND IN OUR WAY.
SHOW ME, GRANDFATHER...
...AND I WILL FINISH WHAT YOU STARTED.

A MAP TO SKYWALKER HIMSELF? YOU'RE RIGHT BACK IN THE MESS.

MAZ, I NEED YOU TO GET THIS DROID TO LEIA.

MMM, NO.

YOU'VE BEEN RUNNING AWAY FROM THIS FIGHT FOR TOO LONG! HAN, NYAKEE NAGO WADDA. GO HOME!

LEIA DOESN'T WANT TO SEE ME.

PLEASE. WE CAME HERE FOR YOUR HELP.

WHAT FIGHT?

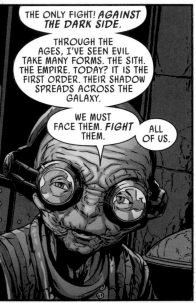

THE ONLY FIGHT! AGAINST THE DARK SIDE.

THROUGH THE AGES, I'VE SEEN EVIL TAKE MANY FORMS. THE SITH. THE EMPIRE. TODAY? IT IS THE FIRST ORDER. THEIR SHADOW SPREADS ACROSS THE GALAXY.

WE MUST FACE THEM. FIGHT THEM.

ALL OF US.

THERE IS NO FIGHT AGAINST THE FIRST ORDER! NOT ONE WE CAN WIN.

SOLO, WHAT'S SHE DOING?

I DUNNO, BUT IT AIN'T GOOD.

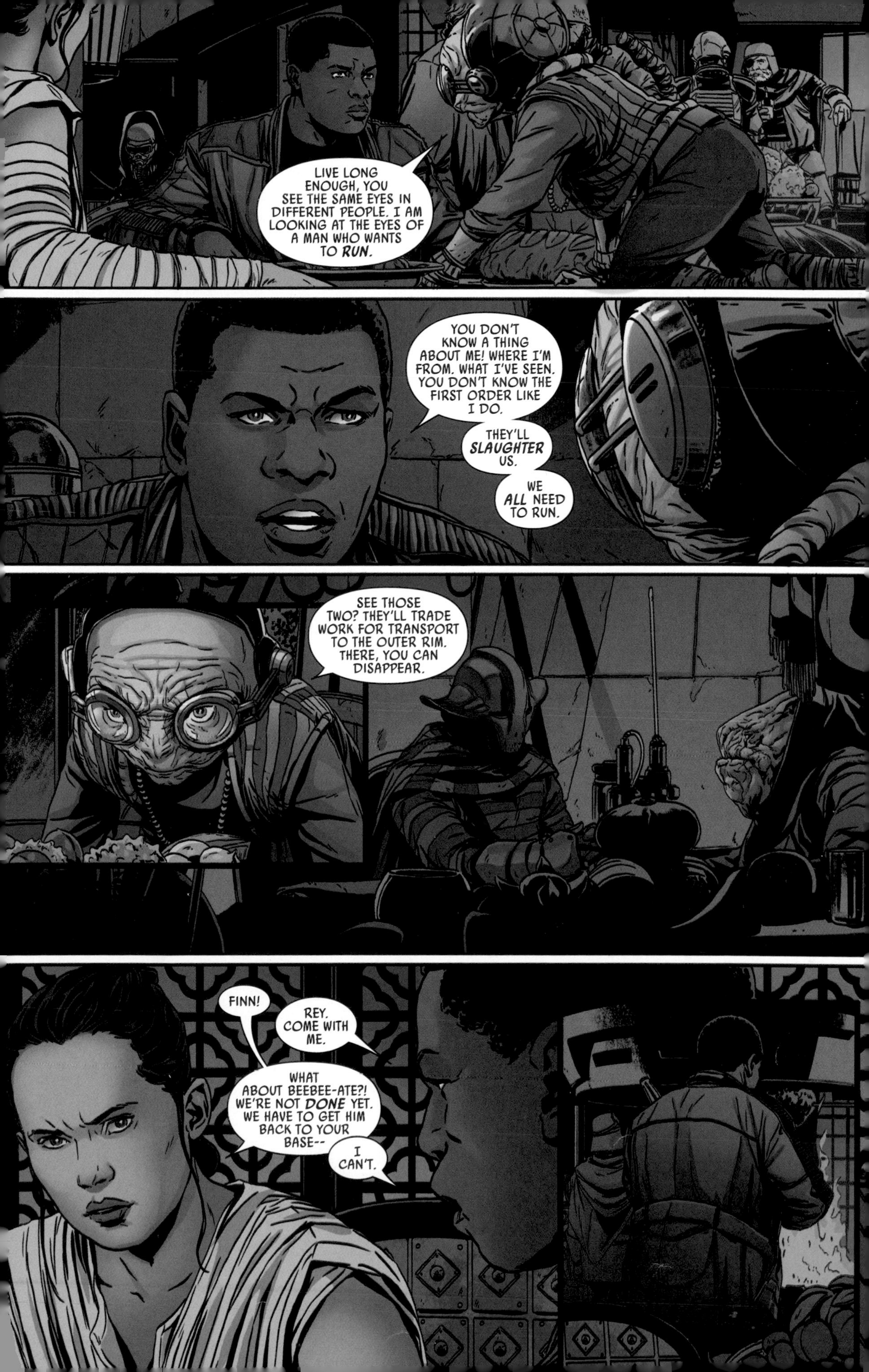

LIVE LONG ENOUGH, YOU SEE THE SAME EYES IN DIFFERENT PEOPLE. I AM LOOKING AT THE EYES OF A MAN WHO WANTS TO *RUN.*
YOU DON'T KNOW A THING ABOUT ME! WHERE I'M FROM. WHAT I'VE SEEN. YOU DON'T KNOW THE FIRST ORDER LIKE I DO.
THEY'LL *SLAUGHTER* US.
WE *ALL* NEED TO RUN.
SEE THOSE TWO? THEY'LL TRADE WORK FOR TRANSPORT TO THE OUTER RIM. THERE, YOU CAN DISAPPEAR.
FINN!
REY. COME WITH ME.
WHAT ABOUT BEEBEE-ATE?! WE'RE NOT *DONE* YET. WE HAVE TO GET HIM BACK TO YOUR BASE--
I CAN'T.

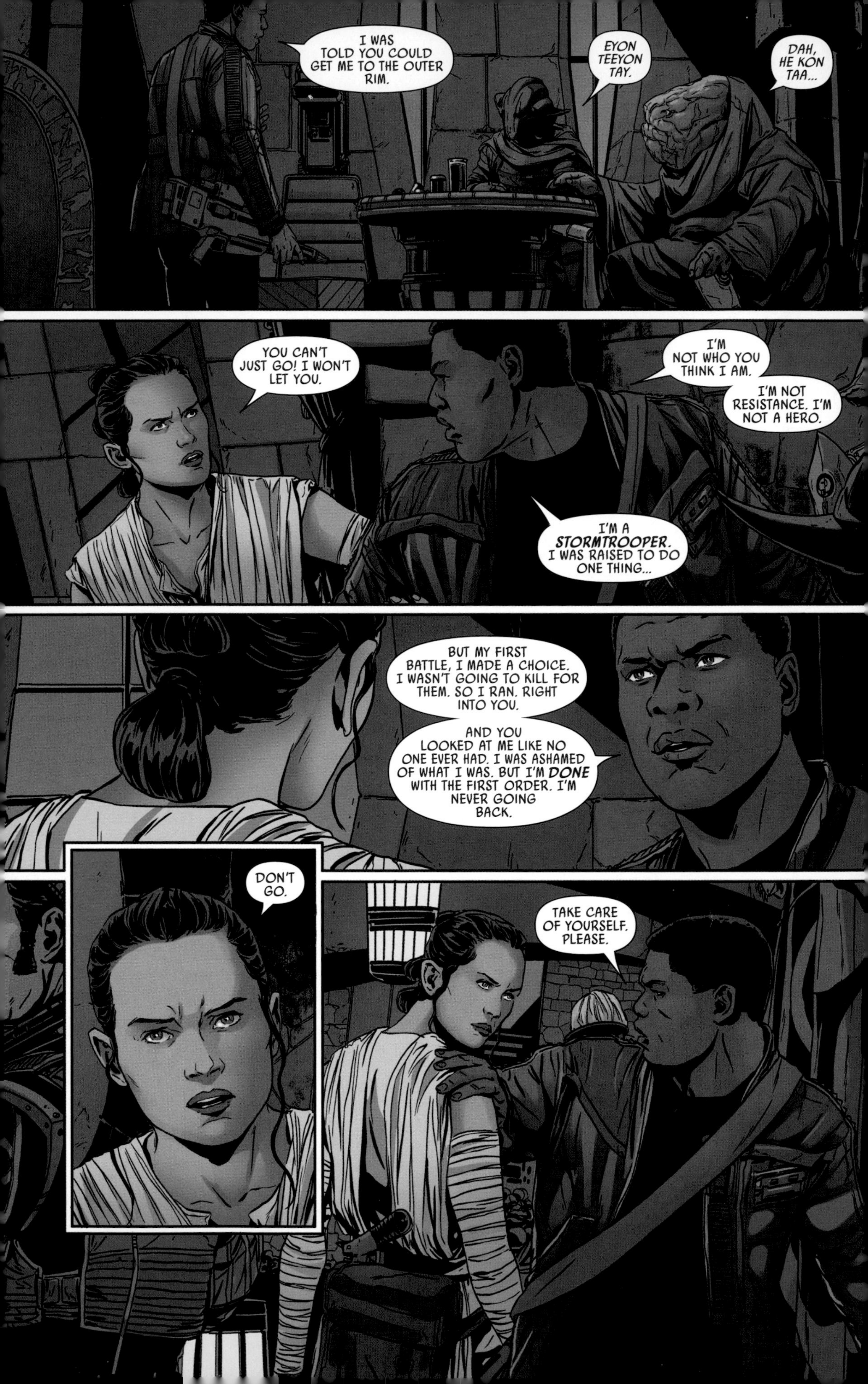
I WAS TOLD YOU COULD GET ME TO THE OUTER RIM.
EYON TEEYON TAY.
DAH, HE KON TAA...
YOU CAN'T JUST GO! I WON'T LET YOU.
I'M NOT WHO YOU THINK I AM.
I'M NOT RESISTANCE. I'M NOT A HERO.
I'M A STORMTROOPER. I WAS RAISED TO DO ONE THING...
BUT MY FIRST BATTLE, I MADE A CHOICE. I WASN'T GOING TO KILL FOR THEM. SO I RAN. RIGHT INTO YOU.
AND YOU LOOKED AT ME LIKE NO ONE EVER HAD. I WAS ASHAMED OF WHAT I WAS. BUT I'M DONE WITH THE FIRST ORDER. I'M NEVER GOING BACK.
DON'T GO.
TAKE CARE OF YOURSELF. PLEASE.

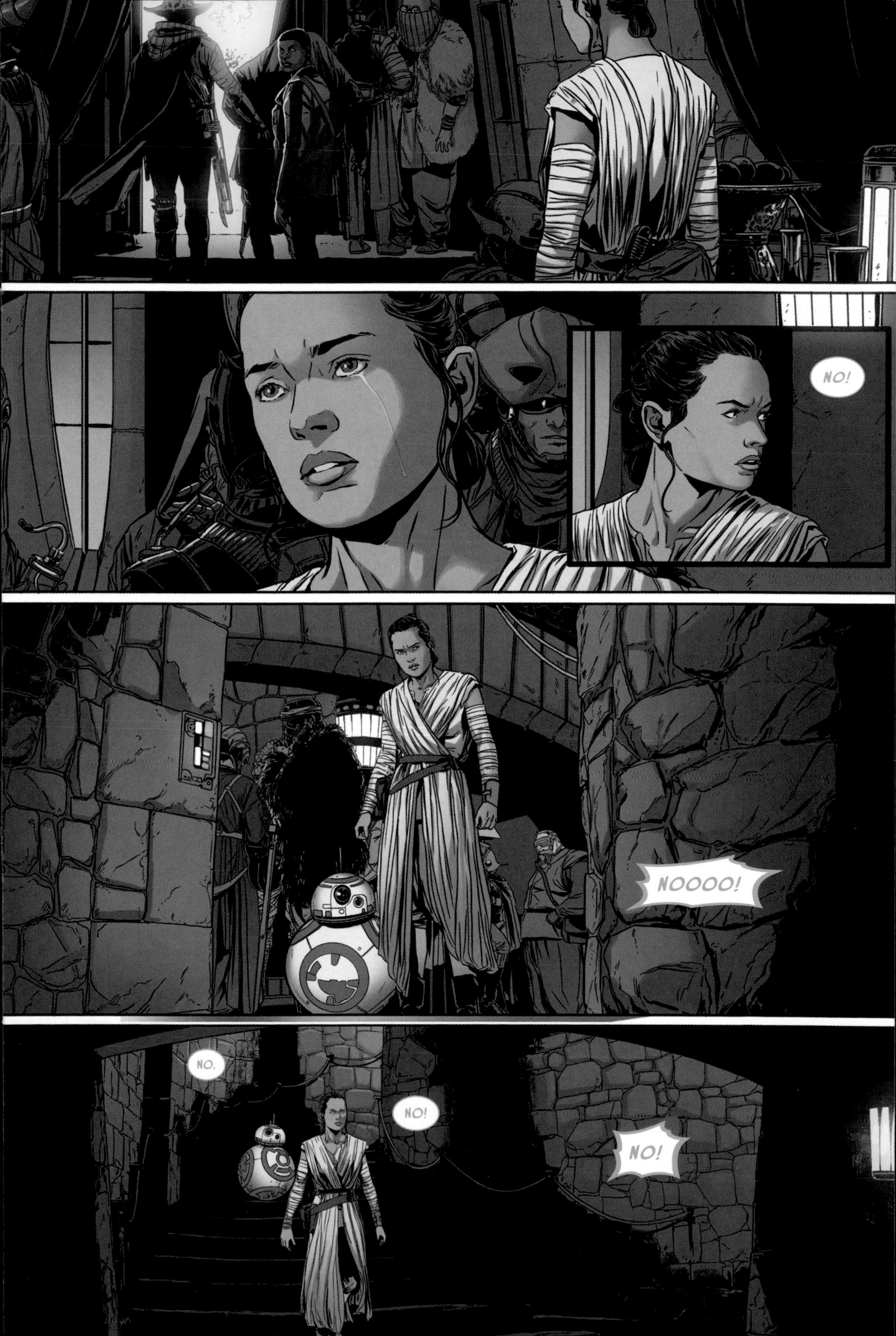
NO!
NOOOO!
NO.
NO!
NO!

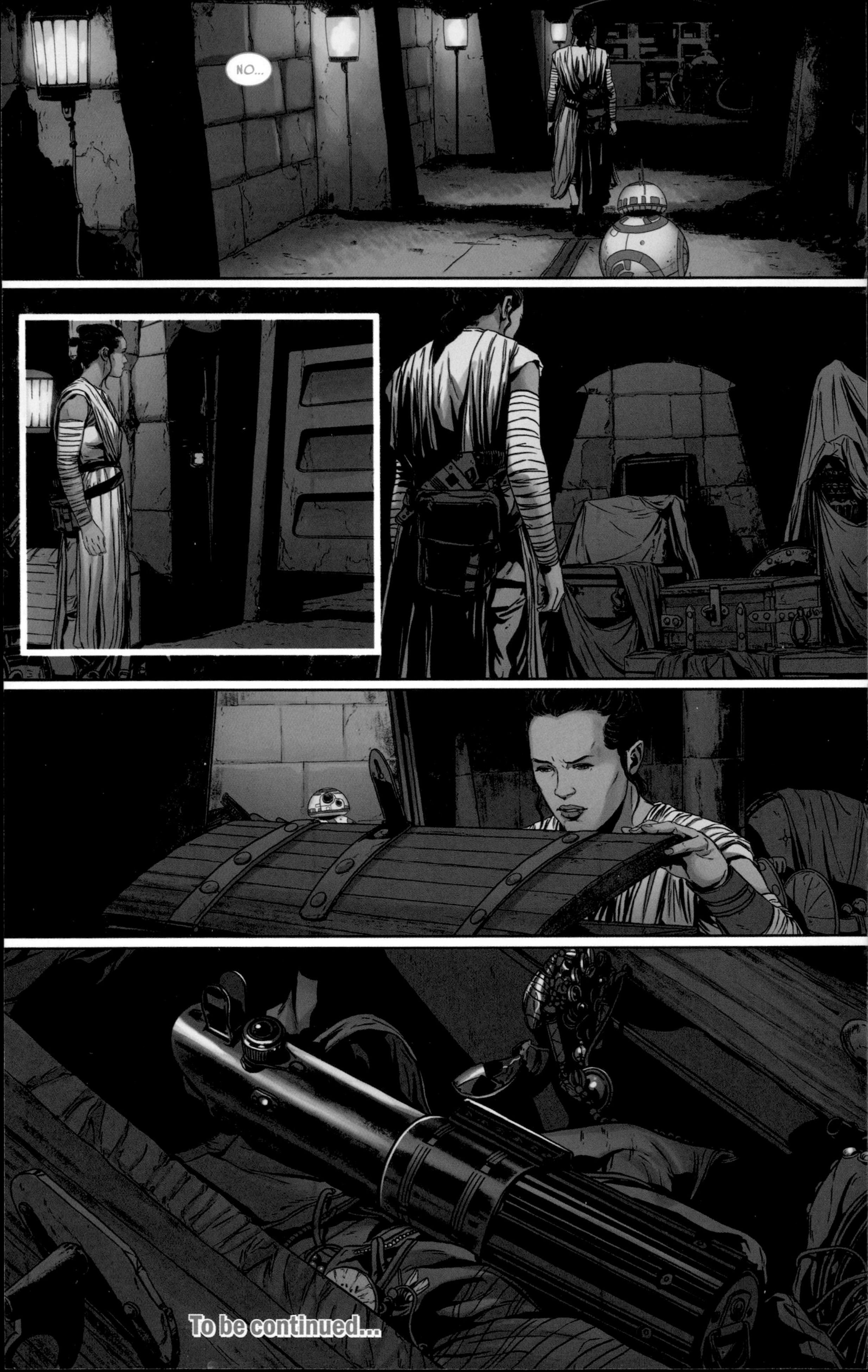
NO...
To be continued...

STAR WARS
THE FORCE AWAKENS
™

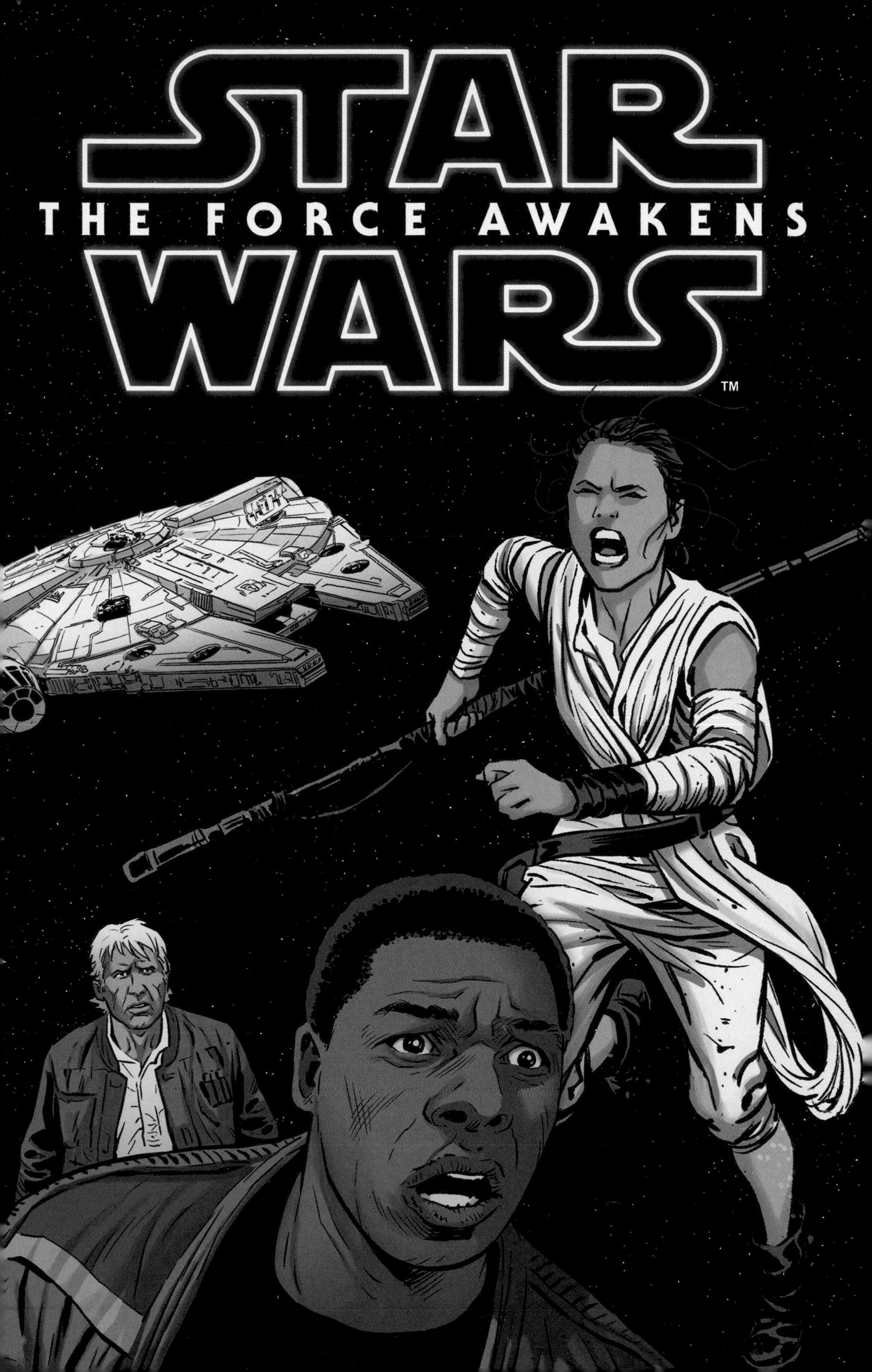

STAR WARS
THE FORCE AWAKENS

COLLECT THEM ALL!

Set of 6 Hardcover Books ISBN: 978-1-5321-4021-1

STAR WARS
STAR WARS
THE FORCE AWAKENS
THE FORCE AWAKENS: VOLUME 1
WENDIG ROSS MARTIN

Hardcover Book ISBN
978-1-5321-4022-8

STAR WARS
STAR WARS
THE FORCE AWAKENS
THE FORCE AWAKENS: VOLUME 2
WENDIG ROSS MARTIN

Hardcover Book ISBN
978-1-5321-4023-5

STAR WARS
STAR WARS
THE FORCE AWAKENS
THE FORCE AWAKENS: VOLUME 3
WENDIG LAMING MARTIN

Hardcover Book ISBN
978-1-5321-4024-2

STAR WARS
STAR WARS
THE FORCE AWAKENS
THE FORCE AWAKENS: VOLUME 4
WENDIG ROSS MARTIN

Hardcover Book ISBN
978-1-5321-4025-9

STAR WARS
STAR WARS
THE FORCE AWAKENS
THE FORCE AWAKENS: VOLUME 5
WENDIG ROSS MARTIN

Hardcover Book ISBN
978-1-5321-4026-6

STAR WARS
STAR WARS
THE FORCE AWAKENS
THE FORCE AWAKENS: VOLUME 6
WENDIG ROSS MARTIN

Hardcover Book ISBN
978-1-5321-4027-3

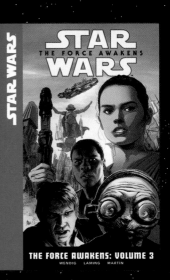

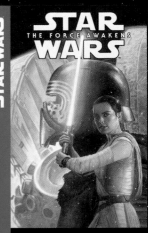